6-95

MAKING THE GRADE · 3

EASY POPULAR PIECES FOR YOUNG FLAUTISTS. SELECTED AND ARRANGED BY JERRY L

Exclusive Distributors:
Music Sales Limited
Newmarket Road, Bury St. Edmunds, Suffolk IP33 3YB.

ISBN 0-7119-2917-3
Order No. CH60006
Cover designed by Pemberton and Whitefoord
Typeset by Pemberton and Whitefoord
Printed in the United Kingdom by
Caligraving Limited, Thetford, Norfolk.

Chester Music
(A division of Music Sales Limited)
8/9 Frith Street, London W1V 5TZ.

INTRODUCTION

This collection of 13 popular tunes has been carefully arranged and graded to provide attractive teaching repertoire for young flautists. The familiarity of the material will stimulate pupils' enthusiasm and encourage their practice.

The technical demands of the solo part increase progressively up to the standard of Associated Board Grade 3. The piano accompaniments are simple yet effective and should be within the range of most pianists.

Breath marks are given throughout, showing the most musically desirable places to take a breath. Students may also need to take additional breaths when learning a piece or practising at a slower tempo, and suitable opportunities are indicated by breath marks in brackets.

THE INCREDIBLE HULK (THEME FROM)

Composed by Joe Harnell.

This theme from the TV series is a wistful and attractive melody, which reflects the gentle side of the Hulk's nature. Try not to cut any phrases short before you breathe.

13
(√)
√
(√)
mf
16
√
1.
19
p
mp
22
2.
√

25
f
mf
f
mf
28
(√)
31
p
p
34

YESTERDAY

Words & Music by John Lennon & Paul McCartney.

Most peoples' favourite Beatles song. Notice the F sharp and G sharp in the ascending scale of A melodic minor (bar 4), followed by the F and G naturals in the descending scale.

A little slower

EL CONDOR PASA (IF I COULD)

Musical Arrangement by J. Milchberg & D. Robles. English Lyric by Paul Simon.

This is a traditional melody from South America, made popular by Simon and Garfunkel.
Keep a very steady tempo.

13
mf
16
19
22
dim. e rall.
p
dim. e rall.
p

SUMMERTIME

Music by George Gershwin.

'Summertime' is probably Gershwin's most famous tune. The notes aren't difficult, but be careful that you play the correct rhythm in bars 11 and 12. Don't let the final D go flat.

13
3
16
1.
19
mp
22
2.
p
dim.
dim.

ITSY BITSY, TEENIE WEENIE, YELLOW POLKADOT BIKINI

Words & Music by Lee Pockriss & Paul J. Vance.

If you want to leave out the spoken sections, you can cut from the first beat of bar 10 to the second beat of bar 12, and cut bar 22 completely. Watch out for the $\frac{2}{4}$ bar.

13
16
19
1.
Two, three, four,
22
Stick a-round we'll tell you more.
2.

BRIDGE OVER TROUBLED WATER

Words & Music by Paul Simon.

Here is Paul Simon's most enduring song.
Try for a full, rounded tone as the piece builds to a climax around bar 23.

15
mf
mf
19
23
f
f
mf
mf
27
rit.
rit.

JEANIE WITH THE LIGHT BROWN HAIR

Words & Music by Stephen Foster.

This song needs really expressive playing.
Be particularly careful of the slurred ninth (A to B) in bar 14. The B should be really soft.

10
√
√

13
(√)
√
mf
dim.
p
mf
dim.
p

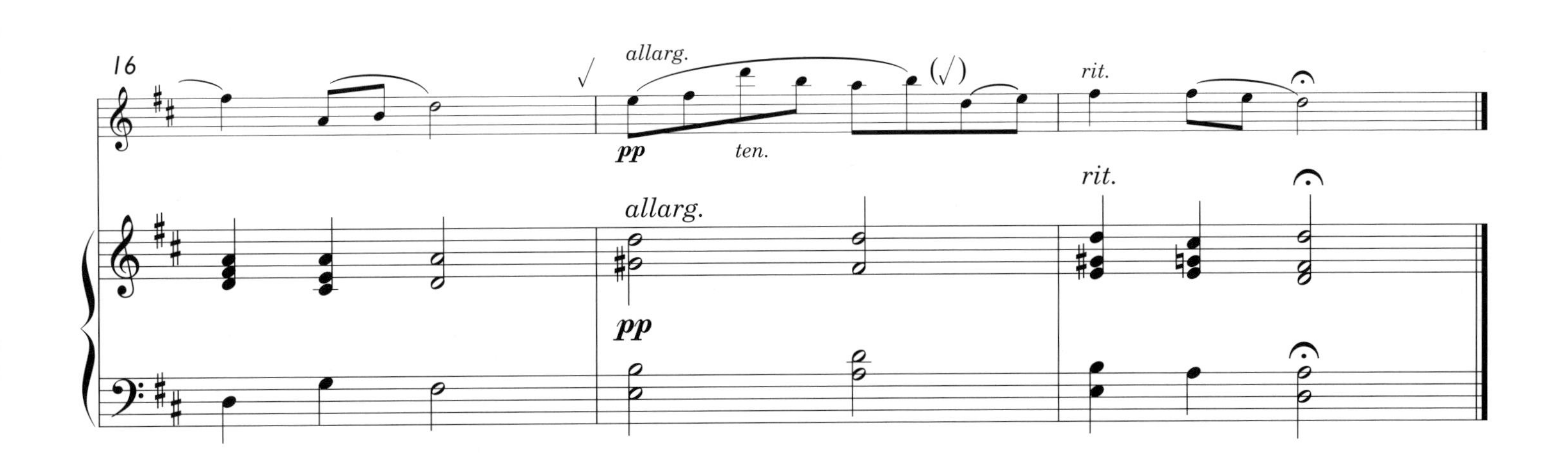
16
√
allarg.
(√)
rit.
pp
ten.
rit.
allarg.
pp

I KNOW HIM SO WELL

Words & Music by Benny Andersson, Tim Rice & Bjorn Ulvaeus.

Many of the notes are slurred in pairs,
which should be practised carefully to ensure that the second note of each pair 'speaks' clearly.

10
1.
2.
mf
mf
13
16
19
rall.
rall.

BIRDIE SONG / BIRDIE DANCE

Words & Music by Werner Thomas & Terry Rendall.

Articulate the quavers in the first section clearly, almost *staccato*, to contrast with the smoothly phrased second part.

14
simile
18
22
26

HE AIN'T HEAVY HE'S MY BROTHER

Words by Bob Russell. Music by Bobby Scott.

Some of the rhythms are a bit tricky in this piece. If you have some trouble with them, practise each phrase slightly slower, counting in quavers. Be careful to count the rests in bar 21.

13
3

17
1.

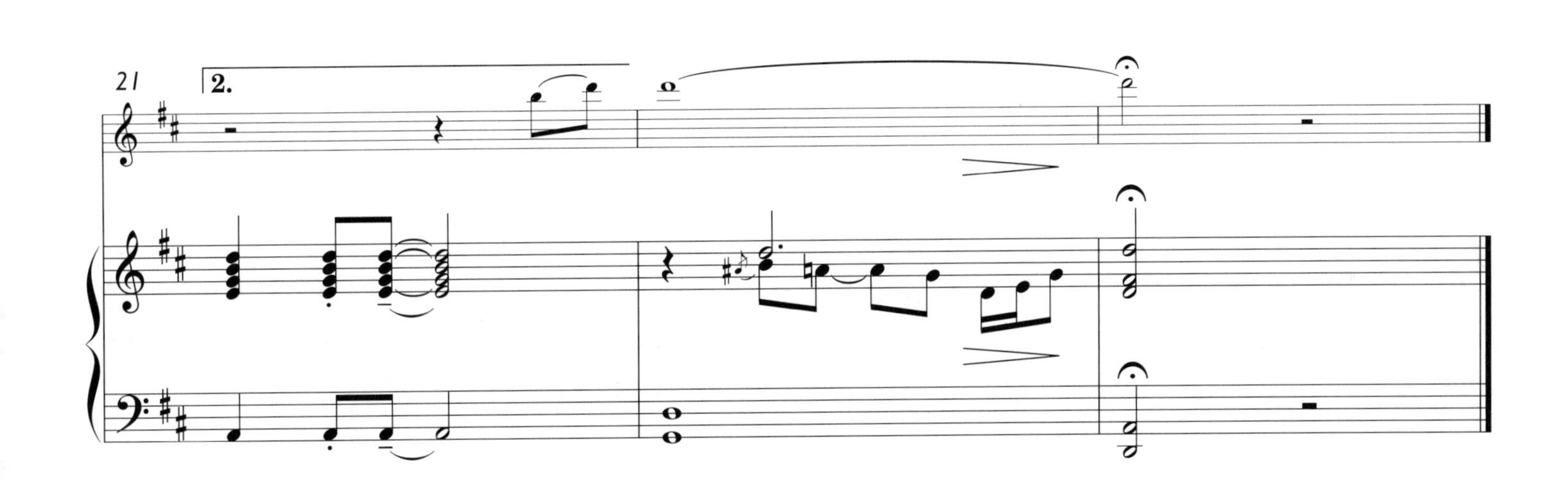
21
2.

AMERICA

Music by Leonard Bernstein. Lyrics by Stephen Sondheim

In this lively number from 'West Side Story' the time signature alternates between $\frac{6}{8}$ and $\frac{3}{4}$; you will need to keep this clearly in mind in bars 17 to 25.

18
23
mf
ff
27
f
f
31
1.
2.

BERGERAC

Composed by George Fenton.

Another TV theme, which here makes a substantial concert piece. The main theme is repeated an octave higher. Remember that D. 𝄋 al ⊕ Coda means 'Go back to the sign, then take the coda'.

18
22
(√)
26
(√)
30
poco f
poco f

34
38
42
to coda
46

50
54
mf
mf
D.𝄋 al 𝄌 coda
Coda
58
mf
61
dim.
p

THE ENTERTAINER

By Scott Joplin.

This piano rag featured in the film 'The Sting'. Make sure you keep a very steady tempo.
You will find that the piece is quite a test of stamina.

13
mp
mp
f
f
16
19
To Coda
1.
2.
mf
mf
23

9/01 (41463)